SAM SWANN'S MO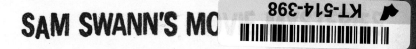

TANYA LANDMAN

ILLUSTRATIONS BY
DANIEL HUNT

**WALKER
BOOKS**

First published 2013 by Walker Books Ltd
87 Vauxhall Walk, London SE11 5HJ

2 4 6 8 10 9 7 5 3 1

Text © 2013 Tanya Landman
Illustrations © 2013 Jay Wright

The right of Tanya Landman to be identified as author of this
work has been asserted by her in accordance with the Copyright,
Designs and Patents Act 1988

This book has been typeset in Stempel Schneidler

Printed and bound in Great Britain by Clays Ltd, St Ives plc

British Library Cataloguing in Publication Data: a catalogue
record for this book is available from the British Library

ISBN 978-1-4063-3086-1

www.walker.co.uk

For Isaac, Jack, Hobson and Sally – without whom
there could be no Sam or Watson

All the chapters in this book are named after movies.
This is how I rate them:

SAM SWANN'S BOARD OF FILM CLASSIFICATION

BG	**BANNED BY GRAN** (Unseen by Sam)	**F**	**FANTABALISSIMO**
FF	**FANTASTICALLY FANTABALISSIMO**	**FFF**	**FANTASMAGORICALLY FANTASTICALLY FANTABALISSIMO**
WTA	**WET THURSDAY AFTERNOON** (Only watch if there's nothing better to do)	**3A**	**AVOID AT ALL COSTS**
W	**WEIRD**	**RS**	**RUBBISH SEQUEL** (Watch the original instead)
5Z	**ZZZZZ** (Sleep guaranteed)	**EPS**	**EYE-POPPINGLY SCARY**
WLI	**WATSON LOVES IT**	**GGG**	**GIGGLES GALORE GUARANTEED**

DEAD AGAIN BG EPS

It's a cold, wet Thursday afternoon. Dad, Watson and I are in Gran's kitchen. Gran is out. If she was in, we wouldn't be doing what we're doing.

Watson is sitting in the corner with his nose pressed to the bin, inhaling deeply. He's staring at the lid, hoping he can force it open with sheer willpower. Canine mind control. There's a bone in there that he thinks will float into his mouth if he concentrates hard enough. I should never have let him watch *STAR WARS* when he was a puppy – it's given him ideas.

Dad is in the opposite corner whistling through his teeth and groping around in a jar of body parts. I am his guinea pig (not literally – I haven't got fur or big teeth and I don't do that *wheep! wheep!* thing). I'm lying flat on my back on the freezing-cold lino, smothered in blood.

Dad's used so much of the stuff that it's pooled around my head and trickled into one ear. The heat from the lights is slowly drying the bloody puddle, so my hair's sticking to the floor curl by crusty curl.

I've been slashed open from my ribcage to just below my belly button. It's not a pretty sight. And I'm hoping that Dad will be finished before Gran comes home and has a heart attack.

Catch!

Dad lobs what looks like a bloodied ping-pong ball right at my head. I can't twist sideways in case my guts slop out. (Not my real ones, obviously. My exposed innards are actually a load of remarkably lifelike latex and silicone organs carefully crafted and positioned by Dad.*)

I don't want to spoil the effect so I stick up a hand and catch the slightly squashy, jelly-like sphere. It's an eyeball. Dark brown eye. Just like mine. Euw.

"Gross," I tell him. "What do you want me to do with this?"

"Put it on the floor there, next to your head. Right in the middle of the blood."

---

* See APPENDIX for instructions. (That's the bit at the back of the book. Not my innards.)

This is tricky because my left eye is waxed shut and smeared with red goo and, like I said, I can't turn over. I nearly give myself a real-life neck injury but manage to get the eyeball where he wants it.

Dad says, "OK, Sam, hold still. I just need a few shots, then we'll be finished. Won't take long, I promise."

I don't believe him. If the last few weeks are anything to go by, I'll be on the floor for hours.

Dad's developing the special effects make-up for his latest movie:

The title says it all. But in case you're still unclear, the logline screams:

ON FRIDAY THE 13TH THE DEAD WILL RISE AGAIN!!!

THE LOGLINE

Every movie has one. It sums up the whole plot in a single sentence. It's how the writer sells the idea to the producer. How they sell it to the money men. It's how the producer of ZOMBIE DAWN!!! got Dad to take the job. He couldn't resist the idea of all that rotting flesh.

In the last few days I've had both arms completely severed, one leg sawn off, all of my fingers broken and my brains blown out. My throat's been slashed from ear to ear. I've been burnt, electrocuted, shot and stabbed. I've also appeared in various stages of decomposition:

Freshly dead

Slightly green about the edges

Beginning to pong

Living walking skeletal nightmare

But before I totally gross you out, let me fill you in on my back story.

A back story. Every character has to have one. Mine goes something like this:

THE LIFE OF
SAMUEL SWANN

My dad, Marcus Swann. Young up-and-coming make-up artist.

My mum, Davina de Silva. Young up-and-coming actress.

They meet.

They fall in love.

They get married.

A year later, I come along. How cute!

Mum is happy being a devoted wife and mother.

Until she gets offered a more interesting role.

She disappears into the sunset with her new leading man.

Leaving me and Dad to get on with things.

It's OK, though. We still see her every weeknight.

8 p.m. Channel 5.

This is me now.

This is my brother-from-another-mother: Watson, my best friend and the most loyal and obedient dog in the universe.

(As long as I've got food in my pocket.)

he second I could talk I begged Dad for a
years, but he finally agreed I could have
my own. We collected Watson on my last
Dad was working on a Sherlock Holmes*
movie at the time so I ended up
naming my dog after Sherlock's
sidekick. I'm training Watson as
a Sniffer Hound so we can solve
Major Crimes together.

HERLOCK ON
SCREEN

So far there have been
147 films made about
Sherlock Holmes. Count
Dracula beats him with
155 – but only just.
The Devil is way ahead,
having appeared in
544 movies!

---
* That is one seriously cool detective.

So far Watson can:

1. Walk
(Not to heel, exactly, but
we're working on it.)

2. Sit
(When I'm holding
a treat.)

3. ...
(Well, that's about it.
We've only done "sit"
properly, to be honest.
But it's early days yet.)

This is my
most essential
piece of kit.

This is Watson's.

We travel with Dad when he's working, but
between jobs we stay at Gran's. I'm home educated.
That's the theory, anyway. Actually, I teach myself
most stuff. Film sets can be boring places and some
days there's nothing to do but read. And it's amazing
how much you pick up hanging around with film
people. It covers all the main subject areas.

<u>On-Set School Report</u>

Name: Sam Swann

Tutor: Dad, I guess

Position in form: 1/1 (yes!)

Subject	Remarks
Geography	We filmed SCOTT OF THE ANTARCTIC in the Antarctic. How cool is that? And HEADHUNTERS OF BORNEO in Borneo. Hot stuff. (OK, so SKINHEADS OF SCUNTHORPE was a low point, but you get the idea.)
Maths	How many film extras can you supply with prosthetic noses on a budget of $50,000?
English Lit.	I'm learning to tell the difference between a good and a bad screenplay. Dad says it's amazing how many producers can't.
Science	Mixing foam latex is a highly complicated chemical procedure, I've discovered. And I can mix the seven different consistencies of stage blood.
English Language	My vocabulary is enormous. I've learnt words that I'm not even allowed to write down.
Art	Helping Dad is very creative. I can make really pointy elves' ears.

Meanwhile, back at Gran's...

EXT: Side of house SFX: Sinister footsteps

Close-up of wrinkled hand with key   CUT TO INT: Kitchen

SFX: Key turning in lock   Sam and Dad exchange look of horror

Dad looks at the mess and all the blood drains from his face, giving him the look of a long-dead corpse. I suppose that's what you call ironic.

Watson gives a loud, happy bark. He forgets the bin, leaps to his feet and bounds into the hall ... over my dead body. My liver and kidneys go scudding across the room and a trail of bloody paw marks gets neatly printed on Gran's white carpet as he gambols towards the front door,
as graceful as a baby hippopotamus.

Gran is not pleased.

And Dad and I can't get the blood out, no matter how hard we scrub.

AIRPLANE! (GGG)

The first location on
the filming schedule
is Romania.

Gran's wearing a big
smile when she waves us
off but I know she's just being
brave. She'll be all alone in her flat,
poor thing. She's bound to miss us.

In the movie industry scenes are never shot in
order. *ZOMBIE DAWN!!!* is being filmed pretty much
backwards, starting with some big crowd shots in an
old ruined castle from the final scene.

"It will be dull," Dad warns me. "Carolyn* says it's
really gloomy there."

"Worse than Scunthorpe?"

"Probably. I hope you've brought lots to read."

I have, but most of it's in my suitcase, which is

---

* Carolyn Styles is the producer of *ZOMBIE DAWN!!!* She's a seriously
  important, seriously scary lady.

sitting in the hold. The flight's delayed and I've finished my book so Dad hands me the screenplay.

Screenplay
The script for a movie, including descriptions of the scenes and camera angles.

The plot of *ZOMBIE DAWN!!!* is basically: an Evil Villain tries to take over the world with a pack of Death Dogs and an army of Flesh-Eating Zombies, led by a Cute Kid. Enter 7¾-year-old child star Tinkerbelle Cherry, who made her zillion-dollar-a-movie name in heart-warming family favourites like *GNOME AT HOME*** and *GNOME ALONE* and *GNOME IS WHERE THE HEART IS*.

Her casting is a piece of genius, because in a horror movie nothing is guaranteed to send shivers up spines more than a sweet-faced kid sucking people's brains out with a straw. Fright Rule Number 1: Nothing is more sinister than a sinister child.

** She got an Oscar for it so she must be a pretty amazing actress.

21

Tinkerbelle's part was originally meant for Bobby Gibson, star of movies like *SUGAR CANDY COWBOY* and *RIDE WEST FOR DREAMLAND*. Any child cowboy part in any movie had Bobby Gibson's name on it. But then something Very Bad Indeed happened to him. You know how food gets stamped with a best-before date? Well, child actors have a cute-before date … and Bobby Gibson's has expired.

He's gone from this: to this:

So the screen writers had to rework the script. The character Edwin has become Edwina and the part's been given to Tinkerbelle Cherry, who, according to Dad, is "a right little diva". I am going to avoid her like the plague.

I read the script through and there are no major plot surprises. Can the hero (Flynn Brightside) rescue his girlfriend (Zara) from the bad guy (Count Dervish) and save the world from Edwina Twilight and the evil zombie hordes? Yes, of course he can. But he's got to slash his way through a lot of bodies first, including Tinkerbelle Cherry's.

Errol Cable as

FLYNN BRIGHTSIDE

Babette Bradshaw as

ZARA

Tinkerbelle Cherry as

EDWINA TWILIGHT

A zillion Romanian extras as

ZOMBIES!!!

Wow! *ZOMBIE DAWN!!!* is a major gore-fest. Certificate 15, at least. There is no way I'll be allowed to go to the premiere. Neither will Tinkerbelle Cherry.

"What do you think, Sam?" asks Dad. "Has it got The L Factor?"

The L Factor: Will it be massive enough to get its own Lego range? Star Wars did. So did Spiderman and Harry Potter. Even Spongebob Squarepants managed it. But *ZOMBIE DAWN!!!*?

"I don't think so," I answer him.

Dad sighs. "No. Me neither."

THE TERMINAL

When we finally land in Romania it's pitch-dark and there's a fierce wind screaming around the airport terminal like some sort of demented animal. It's spooky, so I'm glad we're being met and taken straight to our hotel. We collect our luggage, then head to the oversized baggage area to wait for Watson. Eventually my pack brother comes trundling along on the conveyor belt next to a set of golf clubs. He's sitting in a travelling crate that looks one size too small for him, hanging his head and wearing Expression Number 10: *Deep Misery*.

THE 12 FACES OF
WATSON
1 Happy
2 Sad
3 Worried
4 Hopeful
5 Ashamed
6 Eager to Please
7 Serious and Responsible
8 Listening
9 On the Trail
10 Deep Misery
11 Ready to Play
12 Ready for Bed

When I let him out of the crate, Watson goes ballistic. Four-foot take-offs, cartwheels, laps of honour, the works. I have to keep ducking and diving because if we collide, I know from experience that I'll end up with a nosebleed.

Dad plasters himself to the wall. "Stop it, Watson!" he orders.

But Watson is way too excited to keep still. He's wriggling around as if his spine is made of rubber and he starts

making this little huffling whine that gets louder and louder and he's clearly saying in Labradorian:

I thought I had been abandoned for ever and ever and I was so upset and so worried because I am not a bad dog, no I am not!

I am a good dog, I am an obedient dog and a trustworthy dog and a loyal dog, so you won't ever leave me again, will you, will you, will you? Please please please?

Because I love you
I LOVE YOU
I LOVE YOU
I LOVE YOU
I LOVE YOU!!!!!......

Twenty minutes pass before I can get a lead on him. Then we go and join the queue to get through passport control and all that kind of stuff. Which takes F O R E V E R.

When Watson finally calms down he realizes it's 2 a.m. Way, way, way past his bedtime. He slumps at Dad's feet and falls fast asleep. I sink onto my case and do the same. Every time the queue moves forward, Dad nudges us across the lino. We've hardly advanced at all when another plane lands.

This one isn't your average jumbo. It's a private jet with only one passenger. Well, one passenger and an army of minions. Tinkerbelle Cherry has arrived.

When you're a Hollywood megastar you can demand anything you want. Two hundred pink orchids in your hotel room? Of course. Herbal tea made with leaves plucked at dawn from the steepest slopes of Mount Fuji? No problem. Bottled spring water scraped from one-million-year-old icebergs by Santa's elves? Ask and it shall be given.

Tinkerbelle Cherry's contract says this:

**NO MOON
PRODUCTIONS LTD**

Midnight Studios, 1546 Eclipse Drive, Darktown, CA 666

No Moon Productions ("the Management") agrees with Miss Tinkerbelle Scarlett Wilhemina Cherry ("the Artiste") the following provisions:

i) Management to supply the Artiste with a set of Limited Edition Barbie dolls together with all additional characters, vehicles, houses and accessories as specified by the Artiste in Appendix 73.

ii) Management to supply the Artiste with fifty teddy bears of varying shapes and sizes, brand and style specified in Appendix 74. Required colour for all bears: pink.

iii) Management to supply the Artiste with five long-haired kittens (aged 3–6 months) of tractable disposition, suitable for the Artiste to play with when she is not engaged in professional duties.

iv) Management to supply members of staff to supervise said kittens toileting needs

Real, live kittens! See what I mean? She is one demanding diva.

In her movies she looks like this:

At 2 a.m. in an airport she looks like this:

Bunches

Rosy cheeks

Cute lithp

Floral frock

Sensible shoes

Designer sunglasses

Bling

Designer denim

Designer handbag

Killer heels

While I'm curled up on my suitcase snoring like a pig, the crowd magically parts to let Tinkerbelle through.

I feel a poke in the ribs. Someone's prodding a steel-capped boot into my chest.

I open my eyes to find this staring down at me:

Dad has started to edge away as if he's nothing to do with me. I know what he's up to. It's not the first time he's pretended that we're not related.

Dad is a super-whizz at make-up, so he's dead popular with most actors. But upsetting THE TALENT – in this case Tinkerbelle Cherry – is never a good move. If she throws a hissy fit, he'll be off the movie in the blink of an eye.

I keep my head down and drag my case out of the way – and in the opposite direction to Dad. Watson panics.

As his pack brother, I have violated Rule Number 1: *The pack must stick together at all times*. He whines, he whimpers, he lets out a long, lonely howl.

Meanwhile, everyone's pushing and shoving and trying to catch a glimpse of the starlet. No one even notices Watson.

No one but Tinkerbelle Cherry.

When he howls, she nearly jumps out of her skin. Her sunglasses fall off and she looks around frantically. She seems terrified. Then she realizes it's only Watson and breathes a massive sigh of relief. Weird. She's obviously not scared of dogs, so why did she react like that?

THE RULES OF

PACK BROTHERHOOD

1
The pack must stick together at all times

2
The pack must share:
(a) toys
(b) bones
(c) beds

3
The pack must support each other in all circumstances

4
One pack member must never betray another

5
Pack brothers must watch each other's backs

6
Pack brothers must:
- play together
- roll around together
- eat and sleep together
- bark and howl together

WORKING GIRL BG 3A

By the time we're finally through passport control, Tinkerbelle is probably already tucked up beneath a pink duvet in the penthouse suite at the hotel. Dad, Watson and I go through to arrivals, where a ditzy-looking woman with perilously high heels and far too much make-up is holding up a piece of card with Dad's name on it.

"Marcus, isn't it?" she says to Dad with a grin. No one should be this cheerful at this time of night. "Hi?" Her voice is husky, as if she's got a cold, and it goes up at the end of each sentence as if everything's a question. "I'm Fliss? Fliss Finch?" She sounds like she's not completely sure. "I'm Carolyn Styles's PA's assistant? You know, like, the general gofer? Anything you need, anything at all, you just give me a shout?"

Dad nods and she turns to me. "You must be Sam?" She smiles again and looks like she means it, so I can forgive her for ruffling my hair. Just about.

Then she gets down on the floor and says, "Which must make you Watson? Aren't you a lovely boy? What a nice doggy?"

Watson is all over her but she doesn't let him lick her face, which is very wise because I know the kind of thing my dog eats if he gets a chance and it's not what you want smeared all over your cheeks. Fliss has some crisps in her handbag and she gives one to Watson. He snatches the whole bag and downs it in one. She is now his friend for life.

We all pile into a waiting car. Watson doesn't much like cars so he sits on my lap, which means I can't see anything out of the windows, not even the streetlights.

Dad says, "It's OK about the dog, right? The hotel knows we're bringing him?"

"Oh yes, that's fine? It's a dog-friendly establishment? I made sure of that?"

For the rest of the journey Dad and Fliss talk about the people working on the film, and it's all fairly dull behind-the-scenes movie gossip until Dad mentions Tinkerbelle Cherry.

```
Dad:    We just saw her arrive.
        She looked a bit nervy.
Fliss:  Did she? Oh ... erm...
        Well I'm sure she's fine?
        She's probably just tired?
```

I can't see Fliss's face because everything is blocked out by black Labrador, but I can hear something weird in her voice. So can Dad.

```
Dad:    Is there some sort of
        problem?
Fliss:  No, no, no!
```

Fliss sounds like she thinks she's already said too much.

```
Fliss:  I'm sure things will be fine?
        You can't believe everything
        you hear, can you?
Dad:    What have you heard?
Fliss:  [PAUSE.] It's just that,
        well, there are rumours,
        you know? People say she's
        been a bit odd lately?
Dad:    In what way?
Fliss:  Hearing voices? Seeing things?
```

"Hmm," says Dad. I know what he's thinking. *Great. Perfect. A child star who's going crazy. That's all we need.*

NIGHT OF THE LIVING DEAD BG EPS

When we reach the hotel I follow Dad like a zombie
across the lobby and down endless corridors. By the
time we reach our room I am officially one of the
living dead. I crash onto my bed fully clothed and am
asleep before my head hits the pillow.

I stay that way until Watson decides he needs to go
outside

NOW!!!!!

All of a sudden thirty kilos of dog lands on my chest.
I groan and push him off.

"Dad, Watson needs to go out."

Silence. I prise my
eyelids open. Judging from
the empty bed across the
room, Dad has already
started work. He's left a
note on his pillow with my
work schedule for the day.
Great.

It's 7 a.m. and I am now
Watson's designated Toilet
Attendant.

LESSONS FOR TODAY

English Lit.
Write a poem about
your first impressions
of Romania

Geography
Produce a scale map
of the hotel
grounds

_PE_
Do some exercise

We set off, through corridors decorated with purple
floral wallpaper and swirling orange carpets, looking
for the way out. I'm still half asleep. I don't even
know which floor we're on – but Watson is dragging
me along by his lead. He is a Desperate Dog on a
Desperate Mission.

Then I hear something that makes me stop.

A high-pitched scream, followed by a series of sobs. Then a wail of "Mummy! Mummy!". I recognize that voice from the movies. I'm outside Tinkerbelle Cherry's suite.

I freeze but Watson is frantic to get outside before he has an accident. He jerks me onwards, down a staircase with a big, heavy door at the bottom. I pull it open and Watson bolts out into the grey light of a winter dawn, ripping the lead from my hands and disappearing into the bushes. I follow.

It was Gran who housetrained Watson. She was so worried about her carpets that she watched him every waking moment for more than two weeks. Whenever

he tried to sit down – even if it was just to scratch his ear – she'd launch him into the garden. He wasn't allowed back in until he'd Done His Duty.

Gran had read a book about housetraining; Watson hadn't. He was confused. Sometimes I would catch him looking at Gran sideways, thinking:

She makes me do it outside
and then she brings it back in? Weird!

He thinks Gran is some sort of freakish poo collector. He's learned to tuck himself into corners, sneak under bushes, climb the rockery – anything to make Gran's poo collecting more difficult.

Gran hasn't come to Romania, but that doesn't make any difference to Watson. Pooing in secret has become a matter of Canine Honour.

So there I am – crawling through the undergrowth like a crack commando with a plastic bag in my hand. I'm on Watson's trail and he knows it. He takes evasive action. Doubles back. I cut him off. And now he can't contain himself any longer.

Euw!!!

Mission accomplished.

Double euw!!!

Suddenly feeling a lot lighter, Watson is in the mood to play. I'm not. I haven't even had breakfast yet.

"Food first," I tell him.

The F word. The second it leaves my mouth, Watson's at my side and walking to heel like a true professional. I can do this dog training thing. Simple.

We try to get back in through the same door but it's slammed shut behind us. Brilliant. There are bells clanging inside. Weird. Maybe it's some sort of Romanian custom?

We go round to the front of the hotel only to find a load of guests standing around on the tarmac in their pyjamas. Tinkerbelle Cherry is there in a feather-trimmed pink nightie and fluffy pink slippers. She looks AWFUL – like she hasn't slept at all. She claps her hands over her ears as half a dozen fire engines come screeching up.

Wow! The hotel's on fire! Brilliant!

I stand at the front of the crowd, hoping for leaping flames and columns of smoke and dramatic rescues. Real-life drama beats the movies every time.

The hotel staff are ticking off guests' names and the firemen are running through the building with hoses and then Dad turns up because bad news travels fast and he's heard the hotel's a blazing inferno and come to rescue me and my pack brother.

It's all really dramatic and tense until the chief fireman comes out and says there isn't anything to worry about. No flames. No smoke. Nothing.

According to a guest, who translates, "Some idiot opened the fire door and triggered the alarm."

Dad looks at me. I look at Watson.

How were we supposed to know the door was alarmed?

CASTLE of EVIL 🅱🄶 🄴🄿🅂

Watson and I admit nothing, but Dad decides that he must now Keep An Eye On Us. This is seriously bad news. Film sets are so boring! I'd rather stay in the hotel and watch Romanian TV. I bet I could pick up some of the language.

I explain to Dad that it would be educational, but he insists that we accompany him to Base IMMEDIATELY!!!

> **Base**
> Where the film company parks all the trailers during a location shoot. Like a high-tech caravan site.

Base is in a courtyard perched on top of a hill. The rest of the castle – complete with turrets and towers and a massive portcullis – is across a chasm. You can only get into it when the drawbridge is down.

Once we're in Dad's make-up trailer I head for the swirly-whirly wheelie chair but Dad says, "Don't even think about it. I haven't forgotten what happened at the office superstore."

THE GREAT SPINNING OFFICE CHAIR MISADVENTURE

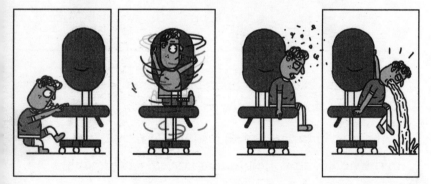

That is so unfair! I was only four. How was I supposed to know what would happen?

Dad maroons me and Watson on a floor cushion in the corner and gets on with his work. All we manage for breakfast is a piece of cold toast between us, which we grabbed from the restaurant as Dad frogmarched us out to the car. It's hours until lunchtime and we're already starving.

Watson is miserable and I am sulking Big Time, but does Dad care? No. He doesn't even notice. He's in an even bigger sulk than me, because while he's been out rescuing us from the not-so-towering inferno, Woody Spiegelman has left him a note stuck to the mirror.

> Marcus,
> Please add a
> scar like this
> to Zombie 197's
> right cheek.
>   Woody

Dad hates it when people mess up his plans. He's like a mad professor, controlling everything down to the tiniest detail; if anyone wants to change so much as a freckle he's likely to freak.

Meanwhile all I can find to read in the make-up trailer is last month's *Star!* magazine. From which I learn:

Lip colour of the season is

scarlet

HAIR EXTENSIONS ARE

SOOOOO

LAST YEAR

Glitter tights are a **must-have** *item*

WHITE - *is the new* - BLACK

RICKI SNAKE'S KILLER HEEL COLLECTION FOR AVANTI IS **TO DIE FOR**

I check my watch. 7.57 a.m. What will I die of first? Hunger or boredom?

LITTLE MISS SUNSHINE 3A

Like I said, the filming for *ZOMBIE DAWN!!!* is starting with the big crowd shots. There are about a zillion Romanian extras (well, 197 to be precise) and Dad's job is to transform them …

from this: into this:

His team have been at it since 5 a.m., but because of the fire alarm incident he's now behind schedule.

 I'm pretty much screaming at the tedium of watching zombie after zombie roll off Dad's production line when there's a sudden commotion outside. Tinkerbelle Cherry has arrived and she needs Dad's full attention. There's only one zombie left to do anyway, so Dad thrusts Woody's note at one of his assistants and makes way for the child star.

Watson spots Tinkerbelle.

Dog + Child = Playtime!

He wags his tail hopefully. Tinkerbelle gives us A Look. Her nostrils flare and the edge of her lip curls.

"Hey, Tinky," says her mother. "You mustn't keep Woody waiting. Hop up into the chair, there's a good girl."

Tinky? *Tinky?* Euw!! Watson and I look at each other. I mime sticking a finger down my throat. Unfortunately, she sees.

I feel bad, until she points at us and says, "What's that doing there? It stinkth!"

Does she mean me? Or Watson? It doesn't matter.

"Sam, Watson, out!" says Dad. One word from Tinky and we're ejected from the trailer. Charming. We have to sit on the steps in the freezing cold while Tinkerbelle-Tinkersmell-Smellybelly settles herself down in Dad's big chair and shuts her eyes, ready to be horror-fied.

The Man Mountain, aka Tinkerbelle's bodyguard, looms over them, cracking his knuckles manfully. Her mum chats earnestly to the stylist about whether they should order the Valentino dress in blush or rose pink.

After a while a stressed-looking Fliss Finch comes along. She smiles at Watson and me, then goes into the trailer.

"Hi, everyone? Carolyn wants to know if you're all on schedule?" She glances at Tinkerbelle's now flaking, rotting skin.

"Almost done," Dad says.

Fliss tries to leave the trailer but Watson blocks her way.

You are the woman with crisps! I am a poor sad hungry dog who will love you for ever and ever and ever and ever if you feed me again, so please feed me NOW because I AM DESPERATE!!!!

Then he starts nosing in her pockets and manages
to pull out a tissue, which he wolfs down before
either of us can stop him. He's so delighted, he's
beating us to death with his wagging tail, so Fliss and
I don't hear Dad telling Tinkerbelle that he's finished
or see her open her eyes, look in the mirror and catch
sight of Zombie 197.

We only look around when we hear

... as Tinkerbelle Cherry, child superstar, falls to the
floor of Dad's trailer in a dead faint.

There's a moment of silence and then chaos erupts.
When Tinkerbelle comes round she bursts into tears.
Pointing at the zombie, she screams, "He's there!

You see? You see him? Mummy!
Muuuummmmmmyyyyyyy!!!!!!!"

The poor zombie's Romanian
– he doesn't have a clue what's
going on. So he's babbling away
but no one can understand him,
and Tinkerbelle's crying so much she's wrecking her
make-up.

It's all pretty dramatic, but here's the really weird
bit: Woody Spiegelman marches over to see what's
going on and everyone's really jumpy because
directors are scary people at the best of times. Woody
denies all knowledge of the note stuck to the mirror.
He didn't write it, he says. No one seems to know
who did.

And no one can say how it got there.

MILLION DOLLAR BABY

Dad throws the mysterious note in the bin, muttering about "time wasters" and "practical jokers". When he's not looking, I retrieve it. It's what Sherlock would do. It's undoubtedly a clue. (To what? No idea. But life on set has suddenly got more interesting.)

Tinkerbelle is given a warm soya milk to soothe her shattered nerves, her make-up's redone, and then they're ready to start actually shooting. Only now does Dad release Watson and me from captivity. He says as long as we stay *on* set but *out* of the crew's way, we can watch.

Being an actor must be the easiest job in the world. The castle drawbridge is pulled up* and all Tinkersmell has to do is stand on the edge of the chasm looking sinister while the extras do their zombie horde stuff in the background.

_____
* They've got this state-of-the-art remote control thingy so they can do it from the outside.

In between each take, Dad and his team have to keep retouching the zombies' make-up and then the zombies all have to go back to their starting positions. And *then* there are the lights and the smoke machine to reset. And if the sun comes out they have to stop altogether because Woody wants everything to look gloomy and foreboding. It's all pretty tedious.

They manage to film a grand total of three ten-second takes before calling for a break.

> **Take**
> A single shot done over and over again until the director is satisfied.

By now Watson and I are practically fainting with hunger. The catering crew has set up a marquee in the castle courtyard and the smell of cooking is driving us both mental. Now, finally, the drawbridge is lowered.

Dad goes off to talk to Carolyn for a moment so Watson and I run on ahead. By the time we get there the place is full of zombies stuffing their faces with hot dogs and burgers, making phone calls, reading newspapers.

Tinkerbelle is nowhere to be seen. She is having her lunch in her own personal trailer, cooked by her own personal chef, followed by some rest-and-relaxation time. I pity the kittens.

I load a plate with chips and rolls and six sausages – two for me, four for Watson – because we've left his dog food back at the hotel.

He wolfs them down in a millisecond. Watson doesn't believe in chewing his food. (Although he's very keen on chewing other things. Like furniture. And Gran's best shoes.) He's looking at me, his big brown eyes begging for more. I'm not allowed to give him any. I'm under strict instructions from Gran not to overfeed him. If he comes back from Romania with even an extra millimetre on his waistline Gran will have it surgically removed.

If she's in a bad mood she'll probably do it herself. On the kitchen table. With a spoon.

I have to sit there and eat while Watson watches me, two strings of drool dangling from his flews.

The lunch break is short because Woody doesn't want to get behind schedule. The zombies soon vanish from the marquee and Dad rushes off to powder their noses.

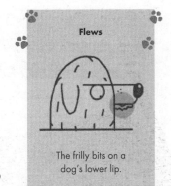

Flews

The frilly bits on a dog's lower lip.

I grab a couple of apples and try to follow but can't. When Watson smells food he acquires the strength of a superhero. He's dragging me in zigzags across the marquee, hoovering up everything he can find. Not just food, either: he'll eat anything. ANYTHING. Sweet wrappers, bubble gum, lollipop sticks, string… I wonder if I'm wrong about the whole sniffer dog/detective plan. Maybe there's another way of making my fortune…

THE CANINE CLEANING COMPANY

The world's first living hoover!
100% spotless or your money back!

DAZZLING RESULTS GUARANTEED!

When I'm finally able to drag
Watson out of the marquee,
they're just about to pull the
drawbridge back up. I don't
want to be left alone in a spooky
castle so we sprint across. We're going so fast, and

Watson is so excited
(superfuelled by sweet
wrappers), that he
pulls the lead out of
my hand. A Labrador
running amok on a film set isn't a good
thing, especially as once we're across he barges into
Tinkerbelle Cherry and knocks her flying. All her
minions rush to pick her up and dust her down and
check her over for injuries. I manage to grab Watson
just as he gets to the edge of the chasm.

And that's when we see the ghost.

GHOULIES

Watson doesn't often growl. He's a friendly dog.
He's convinced that everyone he meets is going to
be his best buddy. I mean, he even wagged his tail at
Tinkerbelle.

So when he does this:

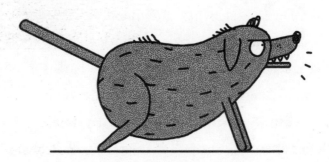

… I know something's wrong.

There's a figure on the other side of the chasm. It
looks a bit like one of Dad's zombies, only I know
for a fact that it's not. Because they're Real and
Romanian. And this one is Freaky and Floating. He's

hovering in a tower window and he's see-through, which is a bit of a giveaway.

It's a ghost. A real live ghost! In broad daylight.

I am *seriously* freaked.

His hair is matted with blood and his head is almost completely severed at the neck. At any moment it might topple off sideways. But that's not what totally weirds me out.

It's the heart-shaped scar on his right cheek.

Watson starts barking to scare off the spooky see-through-man thing. He's defending me.

I'm impressed by my pack brother's courage.

But Dad's furious.

I try to explain, but the ghost has disappeared now so Dad thinks I'm making it up.

Childminders

Nannies

Au pairs

Boarding school

Juvenile detention

Dad threatens Watson with a muzzle and dog-training classes and kennels. He threatens me with all kinds of stuff. Then he sends us both back to the hotel in deep disgrace. Watson and I are now Officially Banned from the set.

If we were in a better hotel it might be OK. But we're in Remotest Romania. The hotel sits all on its own in the middle of a Deep Dark Forest. There isn't so much as a café or a corner shop for miles. And there's no swimming-pool, no gym, no sauna, no hot tub. No Wi-Fi = no online movies or games, no nothing. I've got Dad's list of lesson suggestions but I'm feeling too freaked out and fidgety to write poetry. The TV only has one channel and it's Romanian. I try it for about five minutes but  can't understand a word. How do foreign people manage?

I go to switch it off but then the local news starts and images of Tinkerbelle sliding off her chair and hitting the deck are all over the screen. Someone must have filmed the incident on their mobile.

A child fainting isn't exactly a world-shattering event. If the fainter is Hollywood megastar Tinkerbelle Cherry, however, it's a global news sensation. I feel a bit sorry for her. I mean, I'm in disgrace. But it looks like Tinkerbelle might be in even worse trouble.

YOUNG SHERLOCK HOLMES Ⓕ

I play Kick the Frog for a bit
with Watson. (It's not a real
frog, obviously.) That will take
care of PE, I think.

But our health and fitness programme is interrupted
by one of the maids knocking on the door. She heard
the frog squeaking and thought a small animal was
suffering a prolonged and painful death.

I give up on the hotel and take Watson for a walk instead. I've got my notebook so I can draw a map of the grounds to keep Dad happy.

I can't say I'm loving Romania. Maybe it's a notch higher than

Scunthorpe. Maybe not. It's cold, grey and very, very gloomy. The perfect place to set a horror movie, in fact. Whoever picked this location was a genius.

We're walking in a forest of dark pines, which seems to be the only place I can let Watson off his lead. But it doesn't take much imagination to suspect that vampires and zombies and nearly headless ghosts are lurking behind every tree.

Watson is as freaked as me. He can usually be
relied on to galumph around with insane enthusiasm
the second he's let off the lead, but instead he's
sticking close to my side, breathing anxiously
through his nose. Our walk isn't exactly a happy,
fun-filled frolic in the forest.

When it starts to rain we head back to the hotel.
I can't face another day like this, let alone several
weeks. And while I'm stuck down here, something
genuinely weird is going on up at the castle.

First there was the mysterious note, then there was the ghost. I ask myself: Is there a connection?

And I answer: Haven't the foggiest.

Next question:

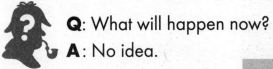

Q: What will happen now?
A: No idea.

6 Eager to Please

"What would Sherlock do?"
I ask Watson.

He looks at me with Expression Number 6. He barks.

"You're right, pardner. He'd investigate, that's what. We've got to get back up there."

For the rest of the afternoon Watson and I lie on the bed and hatch a devilishly cunning plan.

THE *HOUND* OF THE *BASKERVILLES*

(BG) (FFF)

Here are some facts:

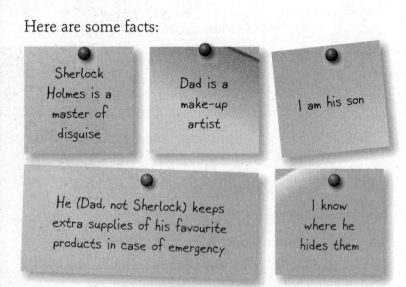

Sherlock Holmes is a master of disguise

Dad is a make-up artist

I am his son

He (Dad, not Sherlock) keeps extra supplies of his favourite products in case of emergency

I know where he hides them

The next day, as soon as Dad leaves for the castle, I pull his secret stash out from under his bed.

I am not the child of a make-up supremo for nothing. In about an hour and a half, I'm transformed…

Strips of wax and latex are stuck all over my face
to make a load of ridges across my cheeks.

The dried strips are sliced open with
a spatula to make it look like my face
has been gashed.

The gashes are painted with
black and red greasepaint to look
like old, crusty blood.

A bit of green and grey greasepaint's
dabbed over that, and – ta-da! –
horror-fied!

Add one false eyeball (one Dad
made earlier). All set!

OK, it's not exactly a professional job, but I figure it's enough to get by.

Watson is more of a problem. I want to leave him at the hotel but he hates being abandoned and I know he'll whimper pathetically until I come back. I have no choice. My trusty sidekick needs to be disguised too.

On Dad's last movie, a Regency romance, he shared a trailer with the lady doing wigs and hairpieces. Sally-Anne was really friendly, and between takes she taught me how to do hair extensions and stuff. I didn't have a human to practise on, so Watson was my guinea pig. By the end of the shoot I could turn him from a Labrador into a poodle in less that twenty minutes.

LESS THAN 20 MINUTES

What's more, I was allowed to keep all the doggy wigs I'd made.

It's just as well I read the *ZOMBIE DAWN!!!* script on the way over. It takes me a while, but I manage to convert Watson from Friendly Black Labrador to …

DEMONIC DEATH DOG

And then we're off, tiptoeing across the hotel lobby, running through the forest and climbing up the 1,426 steps to the castle.

DECEPTION

I can barely stand by the time we get to the castle.
My knees are like jelly. And Watson's tongue's
almost on the floor. We stagger towards the crowd
of zombies looking like we've only just survived a
marathon. No wonder everyone else goes up by car.

I checked Dad's call sheet last night:

NO MOON PRODUCTIONS LTD

Midnight Studios, 1546 Eclipse Drive, Darktown, CA 666

ZOMBIE DAWN!!!

CALL SHEET: 2

Friday 13 September
Cars to ferry cast and crew to location

DIRECTOR:	Woody Spiegelman
PRODUCER:	Carolyn Styles
1st AD:	Cliff Barnes
UNIT BASE:	Drac's Castle courtyard
LOCATION MANAGER:	Lesley Puccini
STUNT CO-ORDINATOR:	Barry Lasseter
SET/SYNOPSIS:	Scene: 93. EXT: Castle. Zombies storm the mountain and exterior courtyard. The drawbridge is raised. Edwina leaps across the chasm.

Cast no.:	1
Artiste:	Tinkerbelle Cherry
Character:	Edwina Twilight
Dressing-room:	Trailer
Pick-up:	07:00
Make-up/Hair:	07:30
On set:	09:00

Tinkerbelle actually gets to do some proper acting today. She's got to lead the zombie hordes in an attack and leap the chasm after the drawbridge is pulled up. To do the jump she's going to be rigged up in a harness and "flown" across on wires. It's an awesome piece of kit. I'll stick around to watch the first few takes. When they break for lunch I'll explore the castle and see if I can get another glimpse of the ghost.

Everyone's getting themselves in place for the first take of the day. I look around carefully, wondering where Watson and I should position ourselves.

1. AMONG THE ZOMBIES?
No way! I'd end up in the film and I don't want to have to explain that to Dad.

2. IN THE TREES?
Possible, but may be too close – I might end up in frame if they do a wide shot.

3. BEHIND THE WALL?
No... I don't think I can lift Watson over it.

4. BEHIND THAT BOULDER?
Perfect. It's close enough to the action for me to see what's going on but I'll be hidden from the actual camera.

I'm heading towards my chosen hiding-place confidently, like I know what I'm doing, and no one's paying any attention until Anne Linker, the continuity girl, spots me.

Curses! She's the ultra-efficient type. Tightly scraped-back hair, flat shoes, no make-up, no nonsense.

She stares, checks her clipboard, shakes her head and comes on over.

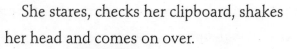

You! Where do you think you're going?

I look at her blankly.

Huh?

Then I have an idea.

The other extras are Romanian, why shouldn't I be?

"I no understand." It's not a very good accent – maybe more Mexican (1) than Romanian (2) – but she doesn't seem to notice.

Instead she repeats herself, slowly and clearly and more loudly, as if because I'm foreign I must also be deaf. "Where … are … you … going?"

I point. "I over there. Same as tomorrow." My accent's flying around all over the place. Now I've slid into Chinese. (3)

"Yesterday," she corrects automatically. She's confused. Checks her clipboard again. "I can't find you on my list."

"Yes." I nod firmly. "I here with death dog. You no remember?" I add – with a great dollop of amazement – "You no write down?"

She's wavering. Everyone in the movie industry

suffers from extreme paranoia. No one wants to be caught doing a bad job – it might be the last time they work.

I hammer in the final blow: "You want me go speak to Woody?" I turn in his direction, but the bluff works.

"No! Go on. Get in position."

So we do. I'm feeling bad for rattling her, but only a bit. I'm not missing this for anything.

CLIFFHANGER (BG) (FFF)

I've crammed a treat box with dog biscuits to keep
Watson happy, but he's wolfed down the lot by
the time Tinkerbelle is finally ready to shoot. She's
running an hour late and I can see she's had a bad
night even before she trips over one of the cables and
falls in the mud.

At least no
one can blame
Watson or me
for that.

She's supposed to look like a rotting zombie, not
a grubby one, so she has to go back to Wardrobe for
a fresh decaying frock. It's another twenty minutes
before she's ready, and by then Woody Spiegelman
is in a monumentally bad temper. Directors can be
pretty weird when they're under pressure and I don't
envy Tinkerbelle at the moment.

"Know what you're doing?" he snaps.

Tinkerbelle nods as Barry, the stunt co-ordinator, straps her into the harness, but she doesn't say anything.

"Tell him what you're going to do, Tinky, sweetie," urges her mother, who's never more than a stone's throw away.

Whatever's wrong, it's affecting her acting skills (which is a Very Bad Thing to happen to an actress). She's supposed to look deadly confident but her voice noticeably wobbles when she answers.

Erm... I stand here. Backgwound action. I look left to wight. Then up at the castle. I run to the edge, scream, then jump across. That's wight, isn't it?

"Sure," Woody says shortly. "Let's get going, people. We've lost enough time."

The technical crew do their stuff and the zombies do theirs and it's sensational. The mist is swirling and the hordes of living dead are following Tinkerbelle. They're climbing the walls, they're going to storm the castle!

Tinkerbelle is about to do the jump – she's taken a deep breath, her mouth's open, her neck's taut, she's going to scream…

But it dies on her lips.

Under Dad's oh-so-carefully-applied make-up she goes a nasty shade of yellowish-green and points a wavering finger across the chasm at the tower window.

"Don!" she cries. She can see something – or someone – so scary that she can barely speak.

But this time Watson's not barking. Not so much as a trace of a growl. Why?

Because there's nothing there. The window's empty. No

ghosts, no zombies. Nada. Zip. Zilch. Nothing.

So why does Tinkerbelle groan and collapse in on herself like a punctured football?

She appears to have lost the use of her legs. This is an Extremely Bad Thing to happen when you're teetering on the brink of a deep chasm. She slips on the scree, overbalances and topples over the edge.

That should have been it. Curtains. The End. Child Star Plummets to a Messy Death. RIP Tinkerbelle Cherry, 7¾.

But she's wearing the stunt harness. It's computer controlled and

Barry's already pressed the button, so this is what happens:

Tinkerbelle dangles helplessly for a few moments before the tech crew manage to reel her in.

The moment she's back on solid ground, everyone erupts. Woody Spiegelman's swearing in about

fifty different languages. Mrs Cherry is screeching and wailing. Man Mountain is ready to thump anyone who gets in his way. The Romanian zombies surge forward to get a closer look …

… and regret it when Tinkerbelle rolls over and suddenly pukes her guts up. Barry's expensive air-cushioned trainers are spattered with the remains of Tinkerbelle's nutritionally-balanced-and-expertly-prepared-by-her-own-personal-chef breakfast. Lovely. The stunt co-ordinator looks like he'd happily throttle Tinkerbelle then drop her body over the edge.

BLEURGH!

Once Tinkerbelle's stopped retching there's a very long, very deep, very awkward silence. No one seems to

BLEURGH!

According to GUINNESS WORLD RECORDS, being sick is officially the most revolting sound known to man! The film THE EXORCIST features a vomit scene that used gallons of pea soup.

know what to say or do. Well, almost
no one. About a dozen zombies have
surreptitiously pulled their phones from
their pockets and are thoughtfully filming
the whole episode.

I have no idea what's going on up here, but there's
one thing I can guarantee.

A delusional, barfing Tinkerbelle Cherry will be
headline news by this evening.

TOWER OF EVIL

You have to feel sorry for the girl really, even if she is a bit of a pain. Chucking up is bad enough, but chucking up in public is even worse. And chucking up all over the Internet (it goes viral in about five minutes flat) ... well, *I'd* be pretty embarrassed.

Tinkerbelle is carried to a car and driven back to the hotel by Man Mountain because she's looking really sick. Carolyn tells her PA to call a doctor, and *her* PA passes the task on to *her* assistant – Fliss – who seems to get landed with

all the bum jobs. She's just heading off to get things sorted when Woody catches her by the arm and says, "Call a shrink, too, would ya, honey? The kid needs therapy."

So Fliss scurries off and Woody calls a break so he and Carolyn and the rest of the crew can rethink today's shoot.

Down comes the drawbridge and the zombies go off to the marquee for coffee and doughnuts. Watson is keen to join them but I don't want to risk running into the continuity girl, or Dad, or anyone else who might recognize me. Head down, I follow the zombies into the courtyard but then drag Watson off to the tower.

Tinkerbelle was looking up at it when she went funny. And yesterday I saw a ghost in there.

Q: What would Sherlock do?
A: Take a closer look.

There's a wooden door with an iron handle so
I pull it open. This is what I find:

The floor has given way in the middle of the room.
There's a big, crumbling hole and I can see all the
way down to the dungeon below. Yikes! There's a
mark in the dust just inside the doorway. It could be
a footprint but that can't count as a clue: ghosts don't
leave footprints.

The floor looks solid enough around the edges of
the room and I really want to get a look out of that

window. Maybe if I stick to the sides I'll be OK. I tell Watson: "Stay."

He doesn't. (We haven't really worked on that command yet.)

So I tie him up and he sits there whining while I go to step through the big arched door.

WHACK!

It's like being blasted in the face by a wizard's wand. The room's protected by an invisible force field! I'm so dazed, it takes me a moment or two to realize there's a sheet of glass across the entrance.

Glass? In the doorway of a tower? What for?

A *MATTER* OF *LIFE* AND *DEATH* (WTA)

Woody decides
to spend the rest
of the day shooting
close-ups of various
zombies, which he'll edit later
and intersperse with the wide-
angle crowd shots. I can't risk being
filmed so Watson and I slip away back
down the steps to the hotel.

Going down is even worse than coming
up; I have the knees of a ninety-year-old by the
time we reach our room. We're sitting on my bed
looking innocent, having done a whole page of maths
problems, when Dad arrives back. (OK, so I haven't

got any of the answers right, but I was pushed for time – what do you expect?)

The news about Tinkerbelle isn't good. The doctor says she's suffering from stress and has signed her off work for a couple of days, which throws everything into disorder. Woody, Carolyn and Cliff are rewriting the shooting schedule. Dad – along with everyone else – is waiting for a call sheet telling him what he'll be doing tomorrow.

Meanwhile, it's time to eat. The three of us head for the hotel restaurant and Dad's barely set foot over the threshold when there's a loud screech of "Marcus, darling!"

Babette Bradshaw has arrived from LA. She swoops across the room to give Dad the most ridiculous series of air kisses you've ever seen. In *ZOMBIE DAWN!!!* Babette gets rescued from the zombies by the hero. But in real life she was once saved from a Fate Worse Than Death … by my dad!

EDITING

This is when the whole film is cut up and stuck back together in a different order. Sometimes half of what's shot gets left on the cutting-room floor.

(Not that the nose made any difference to the results: Tinkerbelle won Best Actress that night.)

Once Babette's finally finished with the smoochie stuff we're allowed to sit down and order some food. Dad has picked a table in the corner so that we can eat in peace. But there's so much gossip about Tinkerbelle that it's hard not to listen in.

Schadenfreude. That's German. Like I said, my vocabulary is enormous. It means "a delight in the misfortunes of others". Dad says the only thing people like more than a successful megastar is one who's falling apart. "They *love* meltdowns," he says quietly to me now. "Look how pleased they all are by Tinkerbelle's illness."

"It's not her fault if she's ill."

"No. But it is her bad luck. And people in this business are very superstitious. They think bad luck's catching – like a cold. She'll be lucky to hang on to the part at this rate."

It seems really mean. Tinkerbelle Cherry's reputation is flopping around like an injured seal. Actors and crew are circling like killer whales, snatching bites out of it. And all because she had … what? A vision? A hallucination? A haunting? I'm not sure. The only thing we can be sure of is that she

saw something no one else did. But so did me and Watson, yesterday.

Although if it's the same ghost, why didn't we see it today? It doesn't make sense.

I'm trying to figure it out but everyone around us is talking so loudly that I can't think properly.

However, that last question is actually a very good one. Directors don't generally risk letting a major talent like Tinkerbelle get anywhere near that kind of danger – the insurance is way too expensive. I ask Dad, "Why didn't they use a stunt double?"

Dad is Deeply Distracted. He's probably thinking about silicone rubber and prosthetic alginate. It takes him a while to register that I've spoken.

"What?"

"Why didn't they use a stunt double today?"

"No idea." Dad looks around. The tech crew are sitting two tables away. Dad calls across, "Barry! Hey! My son's asking why you didn't use a double."

Instant silence. You could cut the atmosphere with a knife. Barry is looking grim. We're talking about the girl that puked on his trainers, after all.

It's Fliss who answers, awkwardly.

"Tinkerbelle asked to do her own stunts? She seemed to think it would be fun?"

Weirder and weirder. Tinkerbelle is into all things pink and fluffy. She doesn't look the dare-devil type. But if she is, what's with the kittens and teddies?

Maybe she's got hidden depths.

Or maybe not.

Barry finally speaks up.

FUN? Is that what she thinks stunt work is? Some sort of game?

He sounds bitter when he says this.

Fliss goes red but doesn't say anything.

There's another long silence and then Barry growls, "You want to know why she's doing it, kid? Come over here and I'll tell you."

DEATHTRAP (WTA)

A back story. Like I said, everyone's got one. Tink's goes something like this:

Mindy Stardrop, aka Tinkerbelle Cherry, zillion-dollar-a-movie child star.

Short and sturdy Don Cardwell, aka Mindy Stardrop's body double.*

---

* OK, so he doesn't look much like her close up, but they're only going to be shooting him from behind, from a distance, in dim light.

THE MOVIE: Gnome Is Where the Heart Is

THE SCENE: Elves have broken into the gnomes' chocolate mine! Cue thrilling chase through the tunnels on a gnomish rollercoaster!

Scene 13, Take 13: something Very Bad Indeed happens. RIP Don Cardwell.

STUNTMAN HARMED IN MOVIE DISASTER!

DEATH ON SET!

FATAL ACCIDENT ROCKS FILM-MAKERS...

Tinkerbelle is devastated.

No more body doubles! From now on, I work alone.

My heart sinks into my trainers when I hear this story. I'm scared to ask what Don looked like in normal clothes, but Barry's scrolling through some photos on his phone. He finds the one he's looking for and hands it over.

"That was taken the day before he died."

A small, fit-looking man is grinning out at me. My stomach heaves. He's remarkably familiar. His head's not hanging off and there's no blood matting his hair, but there's no mistaking the heart-shaped scar on his right cheek.

THE *PHANTOM MENACE* (BG) (EPS)

The story of Don's accident explains a lot. To see someone die when you're only seven is a pretty big deal, especially if his ghost starts following you around afterwards. No wonder Tinkerbelle is weirded out.

We've just about finished eating when Woody's assistant starts handing out call sheets. Dad has to go through tomorrow's schedule with his team, so I take Watson out for a walk before bedtime.

We're barely out the door when he takes off into the bushes. I just have to hope he's not pooing somewhere, because there's no way I'm going to find it in the dark. Or him. I can hear him crashing around so he's probably on the trail of a discarded sandwich or something.

NOTHING!

↓

I'm wandering along the side of
the hotel, thinking about Don, when
I turn the corner and there's the
stuntman himself. About ten metres away. Large
as life. Dead.

He's got a kind of spectral glow to him and he
looks more solid that he did at the castle. Does
that mean he's gaining strength, like the Lizard
in *SPIDERMAN*? What for? What's he planning?
Revenge?

I'm standing there – glued to the spot – when I
hear a despairing wail. Tinkerbelle's in her bedroom
sobbing her eyes out.

"Don!" she shrieks. "Go away! Leave me alone!"

It's seriously spooky. But here's
the mystifying bit.

The ghost is over *there* on the
grass beneath Tinkerbelle's window.
But Tinkerbelle is looking up *there*.
Into the blackness. And I swear
there is nothing up *there* at all.

Which is more unnerving, Tinkerbelle staring into space and *imagining* Don's ghost, or me looking across the grass and actually *seeing* it?

I don't have time to answer that question. Just then, Watson decides he's had enough of the bushes. I don't see him coming, but I feel him thudding into my legs, and I know he's grinning and wagging and saying, "There you are! I haven't seen you for at least thirty seconds!"

Then he notices Don's ghost. A low growl starts up in my pack brother's throat and the ghost turns to look at us. Cold, dark eyes meet mine. The rage in them is terrifying.

I am frozen to the spot. I really, badly want to run but someone's filled my legs with sand.

Watson's barking now and Don's ghost is just staring. I'm half expecting him to chase me like the spooks in *SCOOBY DOO*, or splat me

with ectoplasm like that one in
GHOSTBUSTERS*. Maybe he'll do
an Indiana Jones and blast my skin
off so my blood spills out and only
my bones are left standing.

I have no doubt whatsoever that this is the real
deal. I'm looking at a proper ghost.

Then suddenly it vanishes and I'm disappointed.

There's a loud bang from Tinkerbelle's room – like
her door's been thrown open – and I hear, "Tinky,
darling, was it another bad dream?"

It would have been spookier if the ghost had faded
gradually or whooshed away or at least done some
maniacal cackling. Instead, it was like a light being
switched off. He disappeared in the blink of an eye.

And I was left standing outside in the dark, with the
sound of Watson's barks echoing over the mountain,
and Tinkerbelle sobbing and her mum saying, "There's
nothing there, sweetie. Nothing at all."

---

*   Cool film. I'd definitely rate it FFF. And GGG.

BODY OF EVIDENCE (BG) (3A)

I wish I'd taken a photo. Parents are rubbish when it comes to believing in the supernatural.

Dad's meeting is over and he's relaxing in the bar with some of the crew when I burst in with Watson. I try telling him about the ghost *again* but he just shouts at me for knocking his beer over and then shoos us away without even coming out to look at where I saw the phantom.

"You shouldn't let your imagination run away with you, Sam," he says. Then he adds under his breath, "I should never have let him read the screenplay. It's *THE WITCHES OF WESTLEIGH* all over again."

That is so unfair! It was years ago! My first time on set. How was I supposed to know the witches weren't real? I was only trying to save Dad's life.

SUPERSAM SAVES THE DAY!

It's Dad's fault. He should never have let me watch THE WIZARD OF OZ. I thought witches melted in water.

I stomp off back to our room and get into bed but I don't feel remotely sleepy. I'm really cross with Dad. I *wasn't* imagining the ghost. And it wasn't some kind of glitzy special effect, either. I've grown up on movie sets – I know all about CGI and green

> **Green Screen**
> A neutral backdrop, in front of which actors are filmed. Useful if they're supposed to be flying on broomsticks or falling off buildings. The real background is added in later with computer-generated imagery, or CGI.

screens and stuff like that. This is real, and I'm going to prove it.

But how? How do you catch a ghost?

"What would Sherlock do?" I ask Watson. He doesn't answer. As a sidekick, a dog has drawbacks.

I wonder if I could lay some kind of trap...

a hole?   a net?   trip-wire?   a vacuum cleaner??

But what would I bait it with?

My thinking goes like this: If it's Don's ghost (which it is) and if it's trying to haunt Tinkerbelle (which it seems to be) then Tinkerbelle's the perfect bait.

I need to talk to her. Make friends. (That'll be *hard*. What do girls talk about?)

However tough the assignment, I have to do it. I'll stick to Tinkerbelle like glue. If that ghost appears again I'll be there to see it. Then I'll get a photo, and Dad – and Woody and everyone else – will *have* to believe me.

PLAY IT COOL

"I've come to play,"
I announce as Man
Mountain opens the door
to Tinkerbelle's suite.

He looks at me.

He doesn't move aside.

OK, my plan was pretty
vague but I thought I might
at least be able to get into
the room. How can I stick
to Tink like glue if I'm
stuck in the corridor?

"She's sick, kid," says Man Mountain finally.
"Haven't you heard?"

"I brought her some stuff," I tell him. "To cheer her
up, you know?" I prepared well. Sherlock would have
been proud. First thing this morning I asked myself:

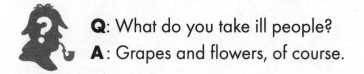 **Q**: What do you take ill people?
A: Grapes and flowers, of course.

So I helped myself to a bunch of grapes from the breakfast bar. And when I took Watson for his morning walk I picked some flowers from the hotel garden. OK, once I'd squished the greenfly they lost some of their dewy freshness, but isn't it the thought that counts?

Man Mountain is unimpressed. "Beat it." He starts to shut the door. I'm tempted to stick my foot in the gap like they do in movies but think better of it. I'd only end up with broken toes.

Then Watson spots
the kittens.

He's not a cat chaser. Well, not exactly. This is what goes through his head:

HELLO, FUNNY-LOOKING PUPPIES!!!
DO YOU WANT TO PLAY????

He barks. The kittens freak. One scampers across the carpet away from the door.

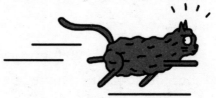

Watson thinks:

WOW! YOU WANT TO
PLAY CHASE! OK!

Thirty kilos of dog launches itself at the door. Unprepared for a Canine Assault, Man Mountain steps back. Bad move. Watson runs into the room and chaos erupts.

Five kittens are shooting off in different directions. Watson can't believe his luck.

Right after the Barbie Dream House is demolished there's a Terrible Silence. The kittens have escaped but Barbie and Ken are buried in the rubble. One plastic foot is sticking out from underneath Watson's

1 Happy

bottom. He's sitting in the wreckage wearing Expression Number 1. He has no idea what he's just done.

Tinkerbelle's mother looks ready to claw me and my pack brother to bits with her blood-red talons. Or to get Man Mountain to rip us limb from limb.

Then into the silence comes an unexpected noise. Tinkerbelle Cherry is giggling.

When she stops laughing, Tinkersmell gives me a long, hard look. She may only be 7¾ but she knows I'm up to something. And she wants to know what.

"Hi, Tham," she says from the depths of her pink duvet. She glances at my dog. "Hi, Watson. Nice of you to dwop in."

Oh, ha ha. Very funny. Although I'm impressed she remembers our names. "Hi, Tinky," I reply. "I ... er ... brought you some flowers."

"What an interesthing bouquet," she says, taking the bedraggled stems. "Put them in a vase, would you?" She hands them to her PA.

"I brought these, too," I say, fishing the grapes out of my pocket.

"You juiced them for me! What a thweet thought."

Ouch! I can see why she likes kittens. She's one hundred per cent cat.

"Did you thay you'd come to play?" she asks.

I've got a bad feeling about this, but I'm on a mission. What can I do but answer "yes"?

"Thuper," she says, throwing back her duvet. "I'll be Barbie. You're Ken."

With Watson tied to the bed leg, I spend the next half-hour reconstructing the Barbie Dream House. Then Barbie and Ken go on vacation. To Hawaii. Bor-ring.

I try to liven things up a bit.

I'm sure Sherlock never had to suffer like this. I'm beginning to wonder if it's worth it. Through the open door Tink's mother is watching us like a hawk, so it's not as if I can even talk to her. I'm on the point of giving up when Mrs Cherry's phone rings. While she's temporarily distracted, I whisper urgently, "I saw it too."

 Tinkerbelle's eyes narrow. She's fully alert. Yep, she's definitely got cat DNA.

```
Tink:  What did you see?
Me:    The ghost!
Tink:  Are you making fun of me?
Me:    No, I'm not! Scar? Head
       hanging off? I saw the ghost.
Tink:  Where?
Me:    Out there. Last night. And at
       the castle before that. You
       saw him up there too, right?
Tink:  Yes!
```

The relief on Tinkerbelle's face is amazing. She looks ready to kiss me. Uh-oh.

```
Me:    Have there been other
       times?
Tink:  Yes. I saw him twice
       in LA. And he was
       outside the hotel the night
       we got here. Mummy and
       everyone else think I'm
       imagining things.
Me:    Well, I know you're not.
```

She's so pleased that she smiles, and I get a glimpse of the zillion-dollar-a-movie star. Even I have to admit it's kind of cute.

But that's the sum total of our meaningful conversation. Because it turns out that Fliss has done what Woody asked and found a shrink – that was who just called. They're on their way up now.

Tinkerbelle Cherry is going to get some therapy.

ANALYZE THIS (BG) (W)

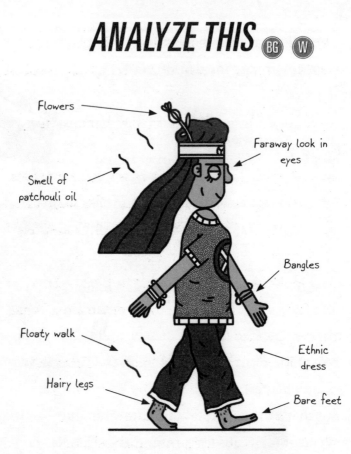

Flowers

Faraway look in eyes

Smell of patchouli oil

Bangles

Floaty walk

Ethnic dress

Hairy legs

Bare feet

If you wanted to cast the part of a psychic hippy in your movie, Zephyr Day would be just perfect.

She waits in the lounge while Fliss comes through to the bedroom to fetch Tink, but Tink's mum is not impressed.

"Who's she?" she asks in a loud whisper.

"Erm ... she's, like, a psychic healer? Woody asked me to get help?"

Tink's mum hisses, "I expected a therapist, not a nut job."

"I made a lot of phone calls?" Fliss's voice wobbles. "But all the top people are booked up? She was the only person I could find who was available, like, immediately?"

"I can well believe it," retorts Tink's mum.

Fliss looks like she might burst into tears, but Tink's PA rescues her. "Give the woman a try. What harm can she do?"

"OK." Tink's mum gives in but now Tinkerbelle throws a hissy fit.

"I won't do it! I won't! I'm all wight!"

"You're sick, kid," Man Mountain tells her.

"You don't want to lose this part, do you, honey?" Tink's mum says.

"No..."

"So we have to do what Woody wants," her mum adds gently.

"He insists?" adds Fliss.

"OK," says Tinkerbelle, fixing me with her cat's eyes. "I'll do it. As long as HE stays." She adds with a flourish, "I inthist."

Thank you very much, Tinkersmell. I was starting to think you were OK but now I've got to spend the rest of the morning doing rest and relaxation exercises. Watson

soon falls asleep but the kittens don't. They keep sneaking up to pounce on him while Zephyr stands over me and Tinkerbelle and teaches us how to breathe.

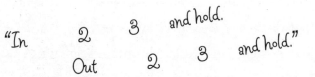

"In   2   3   and hold.
        Out   2   3   and hold."

Does she think we've never *breathed* before? How does she imagine we've survived this long?

Once we're doing it the way she wants, Zephyr moves on to more advanced relaxation.

We're birdies,  flying free.

We're floating in a deep blue sea.

Happy, buzzy bumblebees
sipping nectar.

We're pretty flowers. Clouds.

Rays of sunshine. Drops of dew.

At lunchtime Zephyr says that's enough for today and wafts off in a cloud of incense and tinkly bells. I'm about to escape and dial room service when Tink asks me to stay for lunch. I can't really say no, so I have to endure the nutritionally-balanced-for-a-growing-girl slop prepared by Tinkerbelle's personal chef.

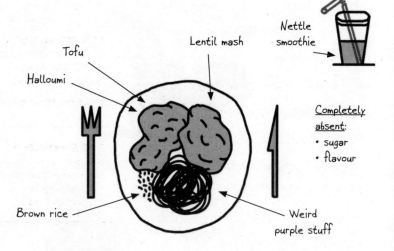

Halloumi

Tofu

Lentil mash

Nettle smoothie

Completely absent:
• sugar
• flavour

Brown rice

Weird purple stuff

I try to feed it to Watson under the table but he looks at it with disgust. Traitor! This is a dog who eats tissues. *Used* tissues! You'd think he could manage some brown rice.

I'm actually considering hurling my plate out of the window when Tinkerbelle suddenly says, "Let's take your dog for a walk."

"What?"

"A walk. Outdoorth. Now."

Her mum intervenes. "Tinky, honey, are you sure that's wise?"

"I just want to see the thun..." Tinkerbelle wheedles. She's got her head on one side and she's looking like those saintly children in old black and white films. Oliver Twist bravely enduring hunger and hardship. SPOILER ALERT! Beth in *LITTLE WOMEN*, dying without a murmur of complaint.

> **Spoiler**
> Something that gives away the plot.

> **OLIVER TWIST U**
> Drama 1948 UK B&W 110 mins
> Orphan boy falls into seriously bad company.

> **LITTLE WOMEN U**
> Drama 1933 US B&W 117 mins
> Four apple-pie-cute sisters grow up during the American Civil War.

"Well, OK, sugar," says her mum. "I guess a bit of fresh air might do you good."

The prospect of a walk has Watson doing four-foot take-offs. The kittens run for cover.

But it takes F O R   E V E R to get out of the door

because Tinkerbelle has to be ready to face the Outside World. She has to look her cutest in case of paparazzi. Her regime goes something like this:

★ ★ ★ A STAR PREPARES ★ ★ ★	
TASK	TIME
Pick an outfit	15 mins
Get dressed	10 mins
Fix hair	10 mins
Stand in front of full-length mirror to check final effect	5 mins

It's forty long minutes* before we finally step outside.

When we get out onto the grass, Watson's so happy that he starts turning cartwheels. Man Mountain hurriedly take a few steps back. Tink giggles so I elbow her and yell, "Race you!"

She's surprisingly speedy. Her mum's calling us and Man Mountain is in pursuit, but we sprint off, up the slope that's outside her bedroom window, Watson bounding along beside us barking his head off.

"Is this where you saw him?" she demands, stopping to catch her breath.

---

* It could be worse. At least Tink's routine doesn't involve using a face cream with nightingale poo in it, like *some* celebrities I could mention.

"No – that's the weird bit," I answer, panting. "He was down there."

Man Mountain has now almost caught us up, so we take off again, down the slope towards where I saw Don's ghost. We're nearly at the bottom when disaster strikes.

Tinkerbelle shrieks and falls, rolling over and over until she crashes into the hotel wall. She lies there, clutching her foot, blood on her hands.

She's trodden on a shard of glass. No, not glass – it's a sliver of mirror. It's gone right through the sole of her pink ballet shoe.

She gets carried back inside, sobbing, and I get sent to my room.

DOGS IN SPACE BG 5Z

Watson and I spend the rest of the afternoon feeling bad. He doesn't like it when people cry (Tink did

2 Sad

plenty of that) and he likes it even less when people shout (Tink's mum did a whole load of that). He lies at my feet looking miserable.

I try to learn the thirteen times table just to take my mind off Tink's injury. It doesn't work. When Dad comes back he's not pleased to discover that we were involved in Tinkerbelle's latest accident. In fact, he's so angry he sets me a spelling test. And after dinner me and Watson are confined to the corner of the conservatory/ bar with a single glass of Coke.

SPELLING TEST
1. Irresponsible
2. Stupid
3. Inconsiderate
4. Insensitive
5. Disappointing
6. Mindless
7. Thoughtless
8. Foolish
9. Reckless
10. Dange R Us

Flat Coke. With no ice or lemon.

Before long Watson asks to be let out. It's raining by now and I haven't got my coat, but this bit of the garden's completely enclosed so I figure I can let him roam around on his own.

I open the door to let him out, then crash down on the sofa and gaze up at the glass ceiling, wondering what's happening to Tink and if the ghost will put in another appearance tonight.

Then Watson gambols across the starry sky.
Uh???!!!!

His outline's blurred and I can see right through him. My dog's died! He's on his way to heaven! For a split second I think I've gone completely crazy.

I'm having hallucinations too.

Then I turn my head and see Watson where I left him, outside the conservatory, tail thrashing from side to side as he truffles up crumbs from the lawn. How

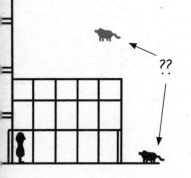

can he be down *here* and up *there* at the same time?

It takes me a few seconds to realize that it's a reflection. Bouncing off the glass wall and up to the glass ceiling.

Glass. There was that weird sheet of glass at the

castle. Tinkerbelle stood on a shard of mirror. Hmm.

I'm still staring up at Watson trotting among the stars when Dad comes over with another Coke for me. He glances up to see what I'm so interested in and says, "Hey! Nice effect. It's like Pepper's Ghost."

"WHAT?" It comes out louder than I mean it to and people turn around to look at us. When they've all turned back again I grab the bottom of Dad's shirt and whisper, "What's Pepper's Ghost?"

"An old theatrical effect." Seizing the opportunity for a bit of home education, Dad pulls his notebook from his pocket and makes a drawing. "It was very popular on stage in Victorian times," he tells me.

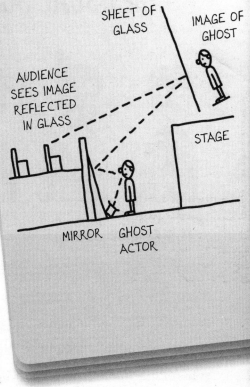

SHEET OF GLASS

IMAGE OF GHOST

AUDIENCE SEES IMAGE REFLECTED IN GLASS

STAGE

MIRROR   GHOST ACTOR

When he goes back to talk to the grown-ups he leaves me with a lot to think about.

Like: Proper ghosts don't need glass or mirrors, do they? Which must mean Don's ghost isn't real; it's a trick. In which case someone must have set it up.

What I can't figure out is who. Or how. Or why.

THE *USUAL SUSPECTS* BG F

PILOT KEN   **BEACH KEN**   *Evening Ken*   **COWBOY KEN**

At 9 a.m. the next morning the phone goes in my room. It's Tink's mum asking me to come up and entertain Tink, which suits me fine because I'm bursting to tell her about the Pepper's Ghost thing. When I get there Tink is lying in bed, her bandaged foot propped up on pillows, with Barbie and Ken enjoying a full-blown fashion show.

Who'd have thought Ken has so many clothes? I mean Barbie, OK, but *Ken*? He is one seriously self-obsessed dude. My fingers get sore doing all his costume changes.

I'm desperate to talk to Tink, but with her mum and Man Mountain in the lounge the whole time, our opportunities for conversation are strictly limited. This is all we manage:

```
Me:    Does your foot hurt much?
Tink:  It's quite thore. But the
       doctor says I was lucky.
       The glath missed the tendons.
Me:    It wasn't glass. It was a
       bit of mirror.
```

We carry on with the catwalk-strutting for a bit, but then I have a stroke of inspiration. I wave Ken in Tink's face.

"He wants to be a magician now," I say.

"He does not!" she cries indignantly, grabbing him.

"Yes he *does*." I grab him back.

"He does not!"

There's a bit of a tussle. Ken's outfit loses a sequin or two.

"He DOES," I say firmly. "It's very IMPORTANT to him."

Tinkerbelle's looking at me with her cat-like eyes.

```
Tink:  Why?
Me:    There's this really neat
       trick he can do with
       MIRRORS.
Tink:  Mirrors?
Me:    Yes. And GLASS.
Tink:  Glath...?
Me:    Yes.
Tink:  I see.
```

So Barbie is Ken's glamorous assistant. I'm tempted to saw her in half, but instead I demonstrate Pepper's Ghost using a pile of books, Tink's bedroom window, a table lamp and the mirror from her dressing-table.

"TA-DAAAAAA!!!"

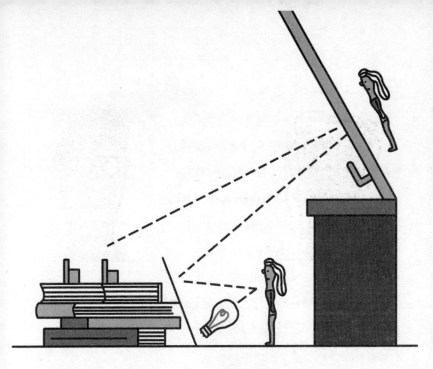

Tink's eyes narrow to slits. If she had a tail it would be twitching. "Thomeone is trying to drive me cwazy," she mutters.

There's silence – I don't really know what to say to that.

"And that explains why thomeone – you, for example – would thee things differently from the side."

She's right! So *that's* why I saw the ghost down on the ground but she was looking way up on the bank – there must have been a sheet of glass up there.

Tink's frowning. She whispers, "But it looked exactly like him."

"Well, that's easy enough, isn't it?" I shrug. "Someone must have used his life cast to make a mask."

My dad has to do life casts all the time, for when he's making prosthetic noses and stuff. One wet weekend he even made a cast of me. (Not that I got to keep it. Gran nearly had a heart attack when she walked in and thought my disembodied head was lying on the kitchen table.)

Don was a stunt double; he was bound to have had a life cast done. It would be easy enough to make a lifelike latex mask from that.

"A mask, of courthe. Very clever," says Tink, looking at Barbie's reflection. "It must have been the thame person who left that note on the mirror."

I'd forgotten about the note but I nod in agreement. Her mum's watching us so I try to act casual as I ask, "Who do you think might have been able to perform such an amazing magic trick?"

Tink glances at her mum before replying. "It must be thomeone who works in the movies. An actor possibly."

"Like who?"

"Thomeone like Babette Bradshaw, for example. Actwesses can get very jealous, you know," she adds in a whisper. "Especially when it comes to winning Oscars."

Babette??

Barry??

Her mum looks over to see what we're whispering about so Tink says in a normal voice, "Or maybe thomeone who worked on a technical crew, like a stunt co-ordinator."

"Barry?" I suggest.

135

"Possibly." Her voice drops so low, I can hardly hear it. "I think he blames me for Don's accident."

Then Zephyr Day arrives and our conversation is interrupted. We try to be flitting butterflies and darting fishes again but our minds are buzzing with everything that's happened. Tink decides she'd rather be a reef shark. Well, if she's a reef shark, I'm a great white. Watson decides to join in too. He's a big blue whale.

When we finally calm down Zephyr says, "I see you're feeling much better, Miss Cherry. I'm glad my healing's working so well."

Tink throws an acid glare at Zephyr's back when she leaves and whispers, "I wouldn't put it past her to be doing all this."

I know actors are paranoid. Dad always says that if you scrape the surface of any of them you'll find a raving lunatic underneath. But Tink is going a bit far.

"Zephyr? Oh, come on! She's helping you!"

"Is she? She's making a lot of money out of it.
First she drives me cwazy, then
she 'cures' me. It would be a vewy
clever plan..."

"She didn't even get to Romania
until yesterday!" I point out.

"How do we know? She might
have been here the whole time."

"Do you reckon? Crikey!" My

Zephyr??

brain is going to start bleeding soon. I can't cope with
so many suspects. Even Sherlock would be stressed.

Mrs Cherry has come in to fluff up the pillows. It's
time for Tink to have a little rest, she says. As I leave
I tell Smellie, "I'll try to find out who perfomed that
magic trick."

"Come and tell me if you discover anything," she
replies. "I'm vewy interested." And the look she gives
me makes me wonder if maybe I'm the only real
friend she's got.

~~10~~1 DALMATIAN~~S~~ (WLI)

It's difficult to find out anything when you're stuck in a hotel in Remotest Romania with no Wi-Fi. I don't even know where to begin. And it's not like I can talk it over with Tink, because she's back on set tomorrow. She's amazing. Woody doesn't want to lose any more time and Carolyn's worried about the budget, so Tink is acting like a true professional and hobbling through the pain.

Dad says they're going for the big zoomy shot of Tink on the tower inciting the zombie hordes to capture Babette and carry her to the castle. Woody wants it done in one long take for maximum effect.

#30861 Zombies storm the castle

From up above we see a swarm of evil ravens circling the castle tower.

Camera swoops through the ravens. Feathers fly.

The small figure of Tink is on the tower, looking over the edge of the parapet.

A brief close-up of Tink at her most evil – arms outstretched, summoning her zombie hordes.

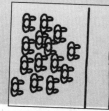

The camera swoops down over her shoulder, over the parapet, taking in the ant-like hordes below. The drawbridge is up.

Camera zooms in on the zombie hordes as the drawbridge is lowered.

And closer. We see they're carrying someone towards it.

Close-up of Babette Bradshaw's terrified face as she's carried into the castle.

I'm not allowed on set and Tink's in bandages so she can't go stamping her foot and inthisting that I'm with her.

But that doesn't deter me – I've had an idea.

There are always members of the public hanging around on the fringes of film sets trying to get a glimpse of the action. Who's going to pay any attention to …

… a little old Romanian lady and her overweight Dalmatian?

"A thpotty dog!" Tink cries through the open window as her limo arrives on set. "I must say hello!"

Tink has seen through my disguise straight away, but maybe she's been keeping an eye out for me. She limps out of the car but Man Mountain is at her elbow in a second.

"Yes, of course you can have an autogwaph!" she says loudly. I haven't asked for one, but it's a clever trick. "Mr Gibbons, go and fetch me a pen."

Man Mountain gives me a hard look but decides that an ancient Romanian granny isn't a security threat. He follows Tink's command.

```
Tink:  Have you discovered
       anything?
Me:    Not yet. Who shall I look
       at first?
Tink:  I don't know. It could be
       anyone.
Me:    OK. I'll keep an eye on all
       of them.
Tink:  Please do. I don't know
       what might happen next.
```

"Tink, honey, come on." Her mum's climbed out of the limo. "You're due in Make-up. We don't want to keep people waiting."

Man Mountain comes back with a pen and Tink signs an autograph for me. When she hands it over her mouth smiles, but her eyes are big and wide and scared. Then she's off to do her stuff, leaving me on the outside feeling worried.

Is she just being paranoid? Or is she in real, actual danger? If driving her crazy didn't work, what else might Tink's enemy try?

DISASTER MOVIE (WTA)

Suddenly the whole set seems fraught with danger. Anything could happen. And it's not just the three suspects Tink and I came up with that I'm worried about. *Everyone* seems suspicious. There are so many ways you could kill someone on a film set!

Will the stunt crew cut through her safety harness?

Are the catering crew putting poison in her hot chocolate?

Is the cameraman going to literally shoot her?

Are the electricians plotting to electrocute her as they lay cables?

I'm a nervous wreck by the time Woody says they're ready to shoot. (Shoot! *Aargh!*)

By now Tink's right at the top of the tower. She couldn't climb the steps so Man Mountain had to lug her up and then leave her there because they don't want him in the frame. She's looking tiny, outlined against the sky, all alone. She must be frightened. *I'm* petrified *for* her.

Keep calm, Sam, I tell myself. Think like Sherlock. (That isn't easy when you're dressed as a granny.) Holmes would find clues. Detect. Deduce. So that's what I'm going to do.

PING!

I'm just wondering where to start when Fliss hurries past me. *Ping!* A light bulb goes on in my head.

I know what Sherlock would do: Ask questions! Interrogate people!

Fliss is the general gofer. She does all the running around. If anyone's going to know something about everyone then it will be Fliss!

Congratulating myself on my brilliant logical reasoning, I call Watson to my side and follow her.

JOURNEY TO THE CENTER OF THE EARTH

Fliss is in a terrible hurry. I don't know what Carolyn's PA is having to do this time, but it involves going down the steps, then ducking off sideways under the rope and edging along a narrow ledge. I hope they're paying her danger money.

I lose her for a moment but Watson's nose is ever-reliable. He knows Fliss is the one with crisps so he's in hot pursuit … and it's then that we discover the secret tunnel.

If this was a movie there would be some seriously scary music playing – like the screeching violins in *PSYCHO* or the "duh dum" shark bit in *JAWS*. You'd be screaming at the screen, "Don't do it!" But it's not a movie, it's real life, so there's nothing to warn us. And if Fliss has gone in there, why shouldn't we?

It turns out to be a long tunnel and I haven't got a torch so I feel my way along the damp walls. It's all a bit *INDIANA JONES* but I reckon if there are any nasty booby traps, Fliss would have triggered them by now.

The tunnel twists and turns and I keep smashing into the stone wall but eventually I see a little chamber ahead. It's dimly lit, as if Fliss has put a torch down on the floor. Maybe it's a dungeon! Euw. Hope there aren't skeletons.

But, no, there's only Fliss, kneeling down, fiddling with something on the floor.

Facing away from us. This is a bad position to be in when you're suddenly spotted by a Labrador, even if he is disguised as a Dalmation.

Hello, Crisp Woman!!

KERPOW!

Watson launches himself at Fliss with joyous enthusiasm and something stomach-churningly disgusting happens.

Watson's mouth is open. Fliss flicks her hair back over her shoulder at the precise moment that he jumps, and her hair gets caught in his teeth.
I think he's just going to pull it a bit, but it's worse than that – he rips it clean off her head. Double, triple euw!!

Fliss yelps in pain and horror. And anger.

I look through my fingers, expecting a red, pulpy mess.

But there's no blood. And the top of her head is covered in dark, cropped hair. *Eh?*

Without all that blonde hair Fliss looks surprisingly, well … *manly*. And faintly familiar.

The clothes aren't right, though. My mind does this:

PILOT FLISS?   *BEACH FLISS?*   *Evening Fliss?*   *COWBOY FLISS...?*

Cowboy Fliss...?! OMG! It's Bobby Gibson!

Bobby Gibson who was supposed to star in *ZOMBIE DAWN!!!* Who is past his cute-before date and now looking *savage*!

And then I see what's in his handbag…

I point an accusing – if shaky – finger. "You're the ghost!"

Fliss/Not-Fliss-But-Bobby-Gibson does a double take because I look like a little old lady, but then he recognizes my voice. "Ain't you a clever kid, Sam?" His own voice has gone from girly to growly.

"But, why?" I demand.

"This is my movie! She stole my part!"

"That's not her fault! You got old and spotty!"

Hmm… Maybe that wasn't very tactful.

Bobby is screeching now. "I could have done it! And I'll prove it – as soon as I get that brat off the movie. I tried driving her crazy, but that didn't work. It's time for Plan B. Twenty minutes, that's all. Then she's toast."

Toast? Where?

At this, Watson starts
ferreting around hopefully.

That's when I notice a clock on the floor – the
old-fashioned sort that goes *tick-tock!* Except this one
looks a bit unusual...

Somewhere above us, Tink
is standing on top of the tower.
And it looks like Fliss/Bobby is
planning to blow it up.

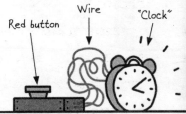

I've got to warn somebody! Do something!
But first I've got to get out of here.

Bobby's blocking the way we came. I try to dodge
past him, but he grabs me. "Over my dead body," he
spits out. He's going to tear me apart!

Only he's reckoned without Watson.

Watson is the friendliest dog in the world, but he's
not stupid. He knows when his pack brother is being
threatened.

When Bobby does this:

Watson does this:

Unfortunately this happens:

Uh-oh. We're trapped underground and no one knows we're here. But at least Bobby can't kill me just now. He's unconscious. And he didn't press the big red button, so Tink is safe. I'm trying not to panic, poking around to see if there's another way out, telling myself things could be a whole lot worse.

Then things *are* a whole lot worse.

Watson decides to sit down and have a really good scratch.

The light's blinking. The clock's *tick-tock*ing. Tink's at the top of the tower with a bomb about go off beneath her.

There's no doubt about it. Things are looking Very Bad Indeed.

APOCALYPSE NOW BG F

My dog has no idea what he's just done. He gets up. Gives himself a good shake. Takes a couple of steps … and disappears. I am seriously weirded out, but then I hear a bark and the clack of claws on rock and I realize he's found a second tunnel. I grab Fliss/ Bobby's torch and follow. It's totally *LASSIE*.

Watson leads me along and down and round and down and along and up and round and up and up and up. It gets steeper and steeper and we both start slipping.

Eventually a chink of light overhead becomes the outline of a square, which becomes a trapdoor. We push it open to find we're at the bottom of the tower – right where I saw that footprint.

My mind does this:

Q: What do I do now? Run for help?
A: No! The drawbridge is up!
Q: Defuse the bomb?
A: No! Don't know how!
Q: Save Tink?
A: YES!
Q: How?
A: Get her off the tower!

So I go up. Up and up and up the steps. I count them as I go. There's this pulsing sound.

vOOM VOOM V[

It's quiet at first but it's getting faster and louder all the time, like the *JAWS* theme. Soon it's thudding. It could be the countdown on the bomb or maybe it's my heart about to explode. Or Watson's.

My legs are turning to jelly, my knees are aching,

my lungs are bursting and Watson's finding it hard
going too. Flecks of his drool are making the steps
slippery and we skid and I graze my knees but we
keep going and all the time that thudding is
getting louder and louder.

At last we're there. 198 steps.
We're at the top.

Watson and I emerge,
wheezing, into the daylight.
Tink is acting her heart out and
I nearly fall back down the steps
when I see her – she's terrifying
in her full zombie make-up.

Then she spots me and
Watson. Is she pleased to see
us? No.

"Get out of the shot!" she
yells furiously.

But I can't see any cameras
or cameramen. So how are they
filming this bit?

The thudding is almost unbearable up here. And there's this strong wind blowing our hair everywhere.

"A BOMB!" I'm yelling at the top of my voice but Tink can't hear me over the thudding.

She sees me panicking, though. I grab her arm. She takes a step with me towards the stairs. Falls. I forgot about her foot. I'll have to help her. 198 steps. How long will that take?

The wind is ripping my clothes. I can't hear anything over the noise. It's deafening.

But I feel the explosion. It's like a soft *pouf!* A vibration. Through the soles of my feet. And a millisecond later, the tower erupts.

THE *END* OF THE *AFFAIR*

Me, Watson and Tink are in the Very Deepest of
Deeply Deep Disgraces. It's ages before they let us
explain what's been going on. It takes the Romanian
emergency services a few hours to dig Bobby out
of the tunnel, and when they finally do he's still
unconscious. But he's OK, and when he comes
round he's carted off in handcuffs to be questioned
by the police. We find out later that they're not too
bothered about his plan to drive Tink crazy but they
are not at all happy about the destruction of one of
their historical monuments. Neither are No Moon

Productions Ltd's insurance company.

While Bobby's in custody he confesses to everything and it turns out – get this – that Man Mountain is his dad! They were working together all along.

Their plot went like this: Man Mountain would text Bobby "SAFE TO APPEAR" every time Tink was alone, and "SCOOT!" every time her mum came running. No one but Tink was supposed see the ghost. The reason I did the first time was because Watson knocked Tink flying and I ended up standing in her place. And the second time – well, they just didn't expect anyone to be out in the grounds at that time of night. On set, Fliss (the general gofer) monitored everything.

She faked the note on Dad's mirror and a whole load of others:

Miss Cherry is to have
the suite overlooking
the hotel garden
                    Woody

Move
mirror
to hotel
garden
        Woody

Move mirror
to castle
tower
        Woody

Place sheet
of glass
in tower
doorway
        Woody

Place glass
on top
of bank
        Woody

They all seemed to be signed by Woody so no one questioned anything.

And that's it. The nice young woman turned out

to be the bad guy. The big beefy bodyguard turned out to be his accomplice. The little diva turned out to be my friend. And Watson and I turned out to be heroes.

Confusing, huh? But that's the way things are in the movies.

That's a wrap!

Edwina Twilight, scary-cute zombie leader
TINKERBELLE CHERRY

Flynn Brightside, the hero
ERROL CABLE

Zara, the love interest
BABETTE BRADSHAW

Count Dervish, the evil villain
GEORGE ROONEY

•••

Producer
CAROLYN STYLES

Director
WOODY SPIEGELMAN

First Assistant Director
CLIFF BARNES

Location Manager
LESLEY PUCCINI

Continuity Girl
ANNE LINKER

Special Effects Make-up Manager
MARCUS SWANN

Stunt Co-ordinator
BARRY LASSETER

Carolyn's PA
GILLIAN WEATHERBY

Gillian Weatherby's Assistant and General Gofer
FLISS FINCH

**NO MOON
PRODUCTIONS LTD**

No animals were harmed in the making of this film.

HOW TO DO AN OPENED GUT EFFECT

1

First check that your client isn't ticklish. It is difficult to apply make-up to a giggling target.

2

Place a sandwich bag or similar item on the client's chest.

3

Cover it with latex (or silicone). Dry with a hairdryer.

4

Repeat this last step several times. Dust with talcum powder.

HOW TO DO AN OPENED GUT EFFECT

5
Cut a slit in the "skin". Carefully remove bag. Raise level of false skin with cotton wool. Apply foundation.

6
Apply black and red make-up to the inside of the slit. Stuff with entrails. The ones you made earlier.

7
Apply copious layers of gelatine to simulate slime.

8
After filming is over dispose of entrails carefully.*

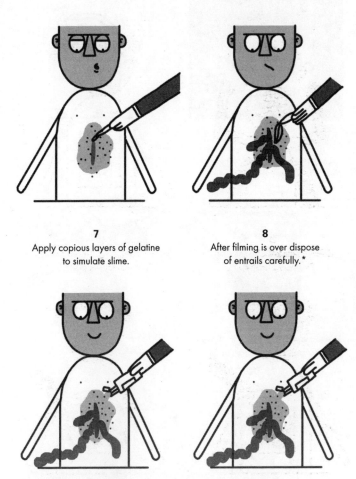

---

* On no account should you attempt to store them in the kitchen cupboard. The gelatine makes them go mouldy. And accidental discovery of such items may upset family members. Especially grandmothers.

DON'T TRY THIS AT HOME!

HOW TO DO A LIFE CAST

1

First check that your client isn't the panicky type. If they're claustrophobic or scared of the dark you might have problems.

2

Smear hair conditioner or Vaseline over your client's eyebrows. (You don't want to rip them off when you remove the mould.)

3

Mix alginate to a nice creamy consistency and gloop it all over your client's face.*

4

Wait for it to set.

5

Make a support shell over the top with plaster bandages, being careful to avoid your client's nostrils. (See (3).)

6

Leave to dry.

---

* Don't shove it up your client's nostrils. You don't want to accidentally kill them.

HOW TO DO A LIFE CAST

DON'T TRY THIS AT HOME!

7
Remove shell and mould. Allow your client to go home.

8
Patch nostril holes.

9
Mix up plaster.

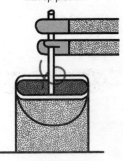

10
Pour it in.

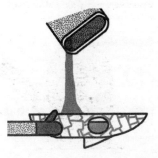

11
Leave to set.

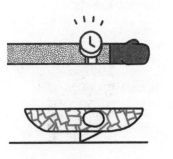

12
Take off mould and paint head to suit.

FILM LIST

DEAD AGAIN 15
Thriller   1991   US   B&W/Colour   103 mins
Logline: Hitchcock-style thriller featuring cool detectives and amnesiac scissor-obsessed mystery woman.

AIRPLANE! PG
Comedy   1980   US   Colour   84 mins
Logline: Disaster movie spoof with plane about to crash.

THE TERMINAL 12
Comedy drama   2004   US   Colour   123 mins
Logline: Man gets stranded in an airport terminal because of problems with a revolution and a visa.

WORKING GIRL 15
Comedy drama   1988   US   Colour   108 mins
Logline: Hacked-off secretary makes it big in business and falls in lurve.

NIGHT OF THE LIVING DEAD 18
Horror   1990   US   Colour   84 mins
Logline: Flesh-eating zombies attack a farm house.

CASTLE OF EVIL (UNCLASSIFIED)
Horror   1966   US   Colour   80 mins
Logline: Family of mad, dead scientist gather in creepy castle for the reading of his will and end up disappearing one by one.

LITTLE MISS SUNSHINE 15
Comedy   2006   US   Colour   98 mins
Logline: Weird family go on road trip.

MILLION DOLLAR BABY 12
Drama   2004   US   Colour   127 mins
Logline: Waitress becomes a champion boxer.

GHOULIES 15
Comedy horror   1985   US   Colour   77 mins
Logline: Demons from another dimension go on a killing spree.

YOUNG SHERLOCK HOLMES PG
Mystery   1985   US   Colour   104 mins
Logline: Young Sherlock's thrilling adventures.

THE HOUND OF THE BASKERVILLES 15
Mystery   1983   UK   Colour   95 mins
Logline: Sherlock treks across sinister moorland seeking the accursed Baskervilles' mysterious dog. (I'm guessing it's not a Labrador.)

DECEPTION 15
Thriller   2000   US   Colour   99 mins
Logline: Ex-con takes identity of dead cell mate because he fancies the guy's pen pal. Euw.

CLIFFHANGER 15
Thriller   1993   US   Colour   106 mins
Logline: Criminal gang crash-land on mountain and need to be rounded up by Sylvester Stallone.

TOWER OF EVIL 18
Horror   1972   UK   Colour   89 mins
Logline: Archaeologists find buried treasure then start dropping dead.

FILM LIST

A MATTER OF LIFE AND DEATH U

Drama   1946   UK   B&W/Colour   104 mins
Logline: Wartime pilot's plane is shot down but he unexpectedly survives and then has to defend his right to live during a court case in Heaven.

DEATHTRAP PG

Thriller   1982   US   Colour   111 mins
Logline: Desperate playwright wanting a hit gets sent a script by one of his old students.

THE PHANTOM MENACE U

Sci-fi epic   1999   US   Colour   132 mins
Logline: Interplanetary wars bursting out all over the place.

BODY OF EVIDENCE 18

Thriller   1992   US   Colour   96 mins
Logline: Woman is accused of killing her millionaire boyfriend.

PLAY IT COOL U

Comedy   1962   UK   B&W   78 mins
Logline: Sixties pop musical starring real life pop legend Billy Fury.

PLAY IT AGAIN, SAM 15

Comedy   1972   US   Colour   81 mins
Logline: Woody Allen gets obsessed by CASABLANCA.

ANALYZE THIS 15

Crime comedy   1999   US   Colour   99 mins
Logline: Mafia boss gets some therapy.

DOGS IN SPACE 18

Drama   1986   Aus   Colour   104 mins
Logline: Struggling rock band Dogs in Space go on tour.

THE USUAL SUSPECTS 18

Thriller   1995   US   Colour   101 mins
Logline: Bad guys do a lot of bad things.

101 DALMATIANS U

Animated adventure   1961   US   Colour   76 mins
Logline: Puppies get kidnapped!

DISASTER MOVIE 12

Comedy   2008   US   Colour   83 mins
Logline: Disaster-movie spoof.

JOURNEY TO THE CENTER OF THE EARTH PG

Adventure   2008   US   Colour   93 mins
Logline: It's a journey to the centre of the earth...

APOCALYPSE NOW 18

War drama   1979   US   Colour   147 mins
Logline: Soldiers journey up the river to attack rebel base.

THE END OF THE AFFAIR PG

Drama   1954   UK   B&W   101 mins
Logline: Doomed wartime romance.

Tanya has written many books for children, including the award-winning Poppy Fields murder mystery series; *Waking Merlin* and *Merlin's Apprentice*; *The World's Bellybutton*; *The Kraken Snores*; and three stories for younger readers featuring the characters Flotsam and Jetsam.

She is excited about her brand-new series, starring the irrepressible Sam Swann and his trusty sidekick, Watson. "I love the movies (it's hard not to when you have an actor uncle who gets eaten by a mechanical shark!*) but I've always been as interested in the backstage stuff as what's on screen. I've got two children – both boys – and two Labradors. Watson and Sam are totally based on them and what they might get up to if they were ever let loose on a film set."

Tanya also writes for young adults. You can find out more about all her books at:

www.tanyalandman.com

---

* Robert Shaw, who played Quint in *Jaws*.